LOVE IS FOR THE DREAMERS

Diana Townsend

"I love the idea of falling in love... even when it doesn't agree with me. There is beauty in the process of loving someone and I crave it... greedily and unabashedly."
Diana Townsend, 2022

Also, By Diana Townsend:

Iced Coffee and Depression: Poetry
Black Girls Evolving: Poetry
Things We Can't Escape: Poetry for the Brokenhearted

CHAPTER ONE:
THE HOPELESS
ROMANTIC

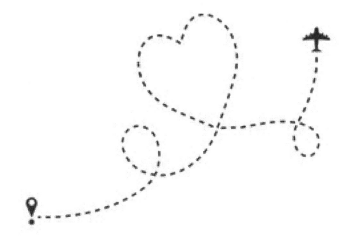

What is this life,
without your arms around me
your lips on mine
our souls intertwined,
and my heart
in your hands?

I trust you to care for me,
to be gentle with my dreaming heart
and what a huge task
to place upon your shoulders...

But you said you were up
for the job
and I am ready
to see how far we can go.

I do not know much about love...
for I grew up in a home that was
built upon a weak foundation,
and arguments were often resolved
with the pounding of a fist.

Please be patient with me
as I learn to love
without toxicity.

You deserve to be cared for
without emotional manipulation
and I am working hard
to give you that
and more.

Please be patient with me.

I was never one
for a lot of affection
simply because
I never received it as a child.

But when you hug me
my body relaxes
and the serotonin rushes through my veins
and I suddenly remember
what it feels
like to surrender
to feel safe
to be held by an angel…
to be loved.

The sun and the moon
aligned and called us together
you, my mighty hero,
broken but not bitter
and me, your goddess of war,
learning to live a life of love
without fighting every battle.

I don't know if I believe in soul mates
but I do know
I would choose you
in every situation
in every lifetime
and in every realm.

When I take my last breath,
your face will be the one I see
as I close my eyes
for the final time.

I would have it
no other way.

People always joke
that you are the good one
in the relationship
but little do they know
how right they are...

For you are the nicest person
I have ever met
with a quick smile for everyone
and a helping hand whenever someone calls
and you never complain
not even in secret
when it's just you and me.

I marvel at your goodness
and thank the heavens
that every night
I can call you
home.

Waking up to your face
sleepy and droopy
the crust in your eyes
as you softly snore...

This is the reality of marriage
and I am thankful for it
because seeing your face
is what gets me through
the long tedious workdays that I dread...

And coming home to you,
as you kiss me goodnight,
and I watch you sleep,
is a secret blessing
that I don't articulate to you
enough.

When it comes to healing
from a broken heart
I have learned that falling in love again
was never the issue...

Falling in love
with someone who loved me
for the person I am
and the person I will continue to grow into...

That has been the issue.

Until I met you.

Promise me,
that when we are apart,
that if things get challenging for you
and life feels troubled
that you will not forget
you are loved beyond measure
and that I am always waiting
for you to return to me...

I will always be
your safe space.

Loving you is my pleasure
it is the sun shining on a rainy day
the excitement of your favorite team
winning in the last seconds of the fourth quarter
the crackle of the fireplace as we toast marshmallows for
smores that remind us
of our childhood and memories
that stay hidden in the deepest pockets
of our minds...

Loving you is appreciating life
in its purest form
and accepting my fate
as being completely
smitten
with you.

The relationships that we hold
close to our hearts
are the ones where we felt safe
to truly take off the masks we wear
to make society feel comfortable…

We can set it down
and just be ourselves
in the presence of someone
who decides each day
to love us for who we are
inside.

He was the first boy I knew
who loved teddy bears
and flowers
for himself
and I smile when I think of him
and his soft delights
because I would indulge them
as often as I could
just to see him smile.

I think my favorite part about you
are the callouses on your fingers
the gentle scratch on my face when you caress me
the reminders of how hard you work
for our family
the gentle way you handle me
and hold me
with hands that have known love
and pain alike.

We whisper in bed
late at night or early in the morning
when we aren't truly awake
but the alarm has sounded
or it's time for bed...

it's in those quiet moments
that we discuss our goals
our dreams
and our fears...

it's in those in-between moments
when we are just two humans
who have learned to love and exist together...

it is then when I love you
the most.

My ex left me
a broken mess crying on the floor
begging him to stay with me
and wondering how I would raise
our child
alone…

You stepped in
and stepped up
loving me and my child
as if we always belonged in your life…

and maybe
in some mysterious way
we always
did.

No one tells
newlyweds
that marriage requires
constant re-evaluation
and check-ins with your
partner.

Neither of you
will be the same people
year after year.

Without communication
the distance becomes
a bridge
tunnels that lead to secrets
and resentment.

I spend my time
at work
daydreaming
about when we can reunite
for the day
and decompress
together.

I feel like an orphan
who has finally found
the stability
that I have longed for
my entire life.

Our signs do not align
we are not compatible with any
of the charts
and yet
the Universe brought us together
many times,
before
we ever started dating.

We would share stories
and realize that we were often
in the same places,
at the very same time,
but we never knew
of each other's presence.

The beauty of us
is that we were going to happen
one way
or
another.

Your love brings out
the very best in me
and I find that I work harder
to make you proud
then I often do
myself.

You reset me
and remind me to take
pride in my work and my accomplishments
for they are my own
and you are just
my humble cheerleader.

I would argue that
you are my muse
and your stamp of approval
is worth my weight
in gold.

What can I do to show you
how much I appreciate
every small thing you bring
to my life…

I've tried verbalizing it
and I thought about writing notes
or write poetry for you
and I've considered
posting about you…

But I am shy
about exposing my heart
so willingly and openly
because I've been hurt before
by men with quick smiles and soft hands
and damaged hearts.

You are different
and it inspires me
to be different as well.

I am going to take a chance
and put it all out there
put it on the line
for you…
because I need you to know
how much you
have changed
my world.

You told me
one cold morning
when I placed my frozen feet
against your body
to steal its warmth
and snuggled close to your back...

You told me that you wouldn't
trade this feeling
for anything in the world
and I smiled my first sincere smile
of the day.

We discovered our love
quietly
but we make it our mission
to love out loud
every chance that we get.

You post me and I post you
and we let the world into
our sacred space
and allow them to believe
in love again
through us.

It brings me a certain level of
vain pride
to see us displayed and packaged
so neatly for the world to see.

You are my pride and joy.

You mentioned
very casually
about the female coworker
who always asks about
how I am doing.

It's so irrational
but it made me uneasy
because I do not trust women
not to see how wonderful and special
you are.

I glance at you
insecure and a little upset
and you laugh your sweet laugh
gently caress my face
and reassure me that
your heart
is mine
forever.

My past relationships
have made me wary
of men who are
too nice
to single women
who do not seem to mind
sleeping with a man
that already has a
happy home.

I am territorial and mean
when it comes to you
but I have also learned
that I cannot control you

and that life has a way
of revealing who we are
inside
whether we like it
or not.

So, I will sit back and trust you
and pray that this is nothing
but harmless interactions
and that you remember
where your loyalties
lie.

CHAPTER TWO:
LOVE ME TENDER

One argument
I did the most horrible thing
and I repeated something
you told me in confidence
and I saw the hurt in your eyes
as I struggled with the demons inside of me
who feed off pain…

Each tear you shed
broke my heart
into a million tiny pieces
and I had to learn
that winning the fight
isn't worth hurting
the love of my life.

I cannot guarantee we won't fight
but I know I will never
stoop that low
again.

That is not how
you deserve
to be loved.

I long for the day
when we have grandchildren
who beg to hear the stories
of our love.

I will relish in the delight
of your sweet attempts to woo me
how you courted me
with flowers and love notes
scribbled on paper in your messy handwriting
filled with your intentions
of making me happy
as long as we both
shall live.

I can't wait to fill their minds
with tales of love and romance
sweet and pure
and with all of the hope
one lonely heart
can wish for
in this lifetime.

Give me all of you
don't worry,
I can handle it
and I have the capacity
to care for your heart
with the gentleness of
fresh morning dew
on a new blooming flower
petal.

I assure you that

my life's mission
is to keep you happy
and add meaning to your life
as you have done
for mine.

Do not ever fear
that you are too much for me
because I am a vessel
prepared to be filled
with the very best
of you.

We have a tender love
and it warms my soul
when I think of you
and my eyes swell with happy tears
because I never thought
this would happen
to me.

I spent so many nights
wishing for a love like this
only to endure
heartbreak and suffering
at the hands of men who
took me for granted.

You worked diligently
to tear down the walls I had built
to protect my heart
and with patience and care
you showed me
what healthy love
felt like.

Kiss me in the mornings
before we drink our coffee
after we eat our breakfast
and especially when we are still
half-asleep.

Hold me into the night
before we drift away into our dreams
after we brush our teeth for the night
and especially when we gaze into each other's eyes
thankful that out of all these people
in the world
somehow,
we found one another.

I secretly enjoy telling people
"I have to ask my husband."
because it gives me a sense of security
that I don't really need
but I sure do love
having it.

In a world where relationships end
and lovers are replaced with new shiny trophies
and profile pictures are swapped out
to eliminate families and memories...

I am thankful for the monotonous
lives that we lead
and the fact that you are always
where I expect and need you
to be.

In the end
I have no idea where our souls
will end up
but baby,
can you promise me one thing?

Fight to find me
call out to me
search for me
and I swear to you
that I will do the same.

Whether we are where the streets are made
of gold
or where the demons cry out
engulfed in flames…

None of that concerns me
as long as I know
where you are
and we can be together
again.

Loving you has been
rich and sweet
decadent to all of my senses
brown sugar and molasses
thick and fulfilling to my soul
enriching my mind...

Our love is an offering
the gods of love
the reward of two hearts
bound together by perseverance and peace...

He is my guarantee
that history
does not always
repeat itself.

New beginnings
are welcome here
and you are the light
that helps my heart
find its way home
after being lost
for so
long.

I manifested a love like this
two hundred times
I wrote down my desires
and requested from the universe:

a partner who would love my mind
before he tried to please my body

a partner who would recognize our differences
and celebrate them as we become a team

a partner who would peer inside my soul
and recognize my good intentions
and appreciate the mistakes that led me
to the place where we are now...

and

a partner who means me well and will give me the decency
of informing me when the relationship
no longer serves them.

Sometimes I fear
you will tire of my anxiety
my constant need for reassurance
the excessive back and forth of my insecurities
my sensitive nature which often leads to
tearful rants...

I feel like I am too much
to deal with
and it terrifies me...

You have been so wonderful
to me
and to lose that
would be a devastating blow
to my heart.

I have no shame in asking
please don't ever
leave me.

Every week
I wake up to fresh flowers
and a small token of love
from you
and it fuels me to push myself
past the depression and past trauma
to believe in love again.

The journey has not been easy
for it is hard to convince someone like me
that your treats are not filled
with poison.

And yet,
you try... day after day.

And this is... love.

Melt into me
seep into my wounds
and heal me from the inside out
please know that this broken shell of a human
has never loved before...

Be careful with me
not out of fear of breaking me
but with caution, as one might have
when exposing someone to something so good
that the threat
of addiction
is
imminent.

I don't think I ever fully believed
fat girls
like me
were worthy of love.

We are portrayed as the sassy friends
good for a quick laugh
and the token comeback…

But when are we portrayed
as worthy of
love?

When I found love
it surprised me
because how could you
love all of this…
all of
me?

I learned that love doesn't require
pity
and
Fat is what I have but not who I am
and love is what I am and not
a dream I must chase
anymore.

You are what I think of
as soon as my eyes pry open
and I begin to stream back into consciousness...

My heart feeds thoughts of you
into my brain
to keep me nourished and well fed
hot soup on a cold day...

You are the material
that is interwoven
in the threads that keep me
together.

I see my beauty
in your eyes
and it makes me believe
in happy endings
and fairytales
again.

I want to soak you up
and absorb every minute detail
of your being...

Allow your soul to crash into mine
and embed the coding of your cells
to unlock the secrets
of the galaxies...

I love you greedily
and it's the only way
that I know how.

My fingers hold the memories
of lovers past
but my heart has the imprint
of you as my favorite
person.

You left an impression on me
and have turned me into a different person
and I will never forget you
and my love language
only speaks your name.

I feel a sense of peace
with you
that hold me together
when I am usually
bursting at the seams
with discomfort and insecurity.

I only have one marriage
in me...
I can only get to know someone
on a molecular level,
one time.

So, this is it
for me,
and I'm okay with that
for, loving you has been
the best decision
of my life.

Do not make a mockery
of this beautiful chance
we have gotten lucky
to experience.

Two souls have bonded
in the sea of billions
and you found me
in all of that chaos.

That is nothing
to take lightly.

I wouldn't mind
drowning in your essence
and immersing myself
into the fibers of your being.

When I daydream about being alone
it's the small things that make me cry
like your scent in the pillows
eventually fading away
or the sound of your voice in the morning
when we sip coffee and eat muffins…

I know I will miss your smile the most
the gentle crinkle of your eyes
as I blush from the intensity of
your undivided attention.

My good news doesn't hit the same
until I can tell you
and see the proud glimmer in your eyes
as you pour your joy into me.

I love how you are always in my corner
supportive and kind
my favorite cheerleader
and the most positive voice
in my head.

You have spoken so much
love and light
into my soul
that my subconscious echoes the thoughts
in my moments of self-doubt.

Inspiration comes in all forms
and you have proven to be
my most pleasurable muse.
I feed off your positivity
as one needs air to breathe
and you nourish my needs
carefully and lavishly
so that I can fall asleep
full of stars and dreams
and safely
in your arms.

Peace is...
sleeping in your arms
the warmth of our bodies
radiating and transferring to each other.

You have a keen ability to understand
that reciprocity is my love language
and as I pour myself into your hands
you fill me with good intentions and
loyalty.

Our cups runneth over
with the nectar
of our love.

Leave the lights on
this time...
I want you to see all of me
as I bare my soul and
strip down my insecurities and doubts...
You make me feel proud of my body
as you take in my curves and dips
and your smile of approval
is all I need
to feel safe.

I do not consider other lovers
for you are more than enough
to fulfill my every desire and want...

It's as if the gods prepared you
with the details and precision
that Michelangelo used to sculpt
his finest sculpture.

You belong to me
and I do not take responsibility
lightly.

The men who came before you
dimmed my light so they could shine
dulled my senses
with their boring conversation
and used me to add a spark to their
otherwise, meaningless lives.

You stimulated every fiber of my being
and slowly became more thrilling than
my favorite book,
more seductive than my favorite song,
and more alluring than anything
I could ever write.

You nursed me back to life
and I escaped a world void of color
once I opened my eyes
and saw love
personified.

Imagine a love
where you can spill secrets
that never gets repeated or said out of anger...

A love that is safe and secure
loyalty is the fine print that you never
have to question...

Imagine a lover who would lose sleep
if they knew you were going to bed
with tears in your eyes
instead of sleeping soundly
while you sob into your pillow...

Imagine a love like this.

Rainy days
spent in bed,
with movies that watch us
as we intertwine with each other.

I call this,
my piece of heaven.

We were so toxic together...
but I would be the worst kind of liar,
a sinner who refuses to repent,
if I denied for one more minute
how much I miss you.

CHAPTER THREE: SOOTHING TO THE SOUL

The thought of living in this world
without the scent of your cologne
lingering on my dress after our morning hugs,
without the sweet taste of your lips on mine
as we kiss goodnight,
without the tingle that skips down my spine
as your body touches mine...

The very thought
drains the color from my face,
for that is not a life that I deem,
worth living,
at all.

You are guarded
because of past hurt
but how will you find the love
that you deserve…
the kind of love that will allow
you to blossom and reveal your innermost
desires and needs…

How will that love find you
if you remain closed off
to opportunities and experiences that
require risk and trust?

Stars shine for us
as we profess our love
with childish innocence
and yell it to the skies
for the world to hear...
At this moment,
we are immune to the doubts
of the naysayers,
we are... invincible.

After one particularly harsh argument
I hung up the phone in angst
and tears burned the wells of my eyes
as I swore, I would never speak to you
again...

I heard the car door slam,
minutes later,
and I rushed to the window
only to see your face, drawn and sad,
determined,
and I ran to you...
a blur of tears and kisses
apologies,
and relief.

Bliss is knowing that all of me
is safe in your hands
as you cup the layers of skin
and self-hatred
that I have despised for so long.

You teach me how to love myself
by admiring me unabashedly
and caressing my body
as if I were a delicate flower
and not the heavy boulder
of depression and anxiety
that I often relate to.

You beat to a rhythm that only I can hear
because real recognizes real
and at the end of this thing
it's you and me
against the world...

and I guarantee
you will win
with me by your side.

I do not spend time
worrying about the opinions of others
when it concerns our love.

We keep our business sacred
but not necessarily secret
it's just time has taught us
that our special moments
are not meant for
commercial consumption.

Once we decided to stop playing
with love
and truly be vulnerable
in the eyes of God
and expose our souls to each other
for our loved ones to see and bare witness...

The heavens showered down
stardust and moonbeams
blessings and sweet dreams
and a love so pure
it could change the world.

I went from an ex
who lied as consistently
and routinely
as the sun would rise

to you...
a partner who understands
that honesty is more admirable
than unrealistic perfection.

What an amazing feeling...
to be loved like this
by you.

He sent me a text
in the middle of my hectic workday
and it simply read
I can't stop thinking of you...

I spent the rest of my day
with stars in my eyes.

Time heals most wounds
and love will heal the rest
when it's with the right person
and the intentions are pure.

Finding this is like finding
a needle in a haystack...
but damn if we don't keep
searching.

Fools rush in
and maybe we were fools
for crashing into each other
shamelessly and effortlessly
without a care in the world.

When you hear our song
I pray that your heart reacts
even if your mind forgets...
Remember my touch,
my smile,
and my love
for you will never know love
like this
again.

This... relationship
brings out the best in me
and you...
reveal the innocence
I once thought was lost
forever.

My inner child feels safe with you
and that says a lot.

Surrender yourself to me
for I know you have been hurt before
and while I cannot claim
to have the expertise
that it would require to heal your
broken heart and guarded thoughts...
I can offer you a chance
to experience love
in its purest form.

It was a lazy Sunday morning
the sun was peeking through
and there was a note on my pillow...

I scrambled to open it
only to reveal the sweetness of your love
written for me to see
and I sighed in relief
because even after all your reassurances
my trauma has convinced me
that you will abandon me.

The heart
is not reasonable or kind
but if we feed it affirmations
instead of lies
then maybe... just maybe,
we will learn how to love with a healed spirit
and not out of need.

I cry a lot...
it's the nature of who I am.
I water my pillows with burning tears of love
and I feel everything...
It's a blessing and a curse,
the life of an empath.

Loving you... has caused the tears
to be soothing and slow
as I cry out in joy and laughter
and allow me the chance
to just... be.

The longest days I ever experienced
were days when my heart
was broken.

The shortest days I ever experienced
were spent in exhilaration
in love and clueless
of the notion that maybe the Earth
spins a little faster
every second that true love
blossoms and takes root
in its holy soil.

In a room with one hundred people
if my eyes were closed
and I could only touch the hands
of those in attendance...

I would still be able
to find you
for I have memorized your touch
and my body would know
eagerly and confidently
that I was back in the hands
of the one who loves me
the most.

Just when I thought it was too late for me
you came around
persistent and kind
and I thought… what if this actually works out?

Every year we celebrate
being together
I thank the gods above
for sending you to me
even though I had lost all hope
of ever being loved.

For what is love
but a fleeting moment of disbelief
and wonder...
that in this world
two people can find beauty and solace
in each other,
despite the odds
never being in their favor.

Coffee and bagels in bed
I lean over to taste the sweetness
on your lips...
these are the moments when time stops
and bliss rises in me
as warm as the morning sun.

Some moments define us
fingers intertwined,
soft lips pressed against each other
in passion and lust...
I pray that you are my eternal soul
my forever person
and in this life
or the next,
I will always find you.
That is a promise.

Touch me
past the layers of hurt
deeper than the artificial film
of a past love that was never meant
to nourish my soul...
Go past the old skin
that has yet to shed...
you will be the only person
to caress my new body.

You are an experience
the Northern lights on a clear black night
the eighth wonder of the world
my lucky ticket
the extra sip of the drink in an almost empty cup
my favorite scent
a shot of adrenaline
in an otherwise blurry and dull world.

Girls spend their time worrying
and fretting over love
while boys play the field
and worry over impressing their friends…

Once I found a man
who prioritized communication and loyalty
over childish games,
it opened my eyes and I saw the world
with a renewed lease on life.

I wish for a love
that eases into my heart
with the gentle drums of passion
slow and steady
consistent and reliable...
I crave the solid foundation
of trust.

Imagine learning to trust again
after your heart has been broken
and you wondered how you would ever take
another breath…

You deserve to love again
and experience all that the world
has to offer
without settling for less.

Let's admit it...
You can be happy alone,
but the world is just a little sweeter,
the sky seems a little bluer,
the flowers smell sweeter,
your smile is a little wider,
and your heart beats a little faster...
when you are in love.

This high is what we chase.

There is something sensual
about kissing...
something that transcends time
and souls intertwine
even if they aren't meant to be.

This is why I am selfish with my kisses...
and I save them for those I truly love.
I have no desire to share my innermost self...
with random people
who are blinded to the beauty
of my love.

Ocean views
wrapped in blankets on the balcony
we snuggle, warm and tingly,
listening to the crash of the waves
and the giggles of the oblivious kids below...

We stay out until the moon hovers over us
our bodies soft and heavy
drunk with wine and love
our breathing begins to syncopate
and our hearts race
to the finish line.

Do you believe in true love?

It's whimsical and silly
the thought that one person could be
the answer to our prayers and make
all of our dreams come true...

and yet, what would life be
without the hope of waking up
to the same soul
every single day,
and know they are yours,
and yours alone...

The thought alone
is definitely my drug of choice.

There is a sense of ease
when we are together...
this sensation that I can be my nerdy self
with you
or my goofy self
the version of myself that is usually silenced
by the annoyance of others
who claim to enjoy my presence as long
as it fits their narrative...

I get to be comfortable with you...

There is safety
in your love
and damn…
I appreciate that
with my whole heart.

Giving more of myself
never feels like a chore
when you are around...

I adore your willingness to receive
wholeheartedly and openly
and you reciprocate my love
with a smile...

It's an even exchange of pleasure
that I do not take
for granted.

Loving myself doesn't feel like a chore
and it allows me to set the expectations
for how I expect to be loved by you…

I will not accept the bare minimum
from anyone else
when I love to go above and beyond
for myself.

Are you willing to try?

It would mean having an exceptional
amount of patience
and a significant amount of
forgiveness
and a daily dose of kindness...

We cannot find our way back to each other
without a daily commitment
to seek each other out
every moment,
of every day.

I require softness
for my heart is beaten and tattered
hanging on by a thin string
of hope
that you will be different
from the rest.

Healed love requires
therapy
honesty
self-care
space
kindness
and
inner peace.

Please do not engage with anyone
asking to be loved
if you are not prepared
to equip the necessary tools.

ACKNOWLEDGEMENT

I am deeply grateful to my mother for her unwavering support throughout my journey as a writer. My husband and daughter, who have been my source of love and joy, have also been my biggest cheerleaders. My sisters, who have always been there for me, have also played a significant role in my life. Lastly, I would like to express my sincere gratitude to my readers, who have made this journey so fulfilling and meaningful. Thank you all from the bottom of my heart.

ABOUT THE AUTHOR

Diana Townsend

Diana Townsend is an avid reader and writer who finds joy in the small things in life. She loves to explore the world through the written word, both in the books she reads and in her writing. With a keen eye for detail and a passion for storytelling, she weaves together tales that captivate and delight readers of all ages. Whether you're looking for heartfelt poetry, a sweet children's book, or a thought-provoking read, you'll find it in her work. With her writing, Diana wants to remind people of the beauty and wonder that surrounds us, and the importance of cherishing the small things in life.

Made in the USA
Middletown, DE
27 March 2023

27812812R00068